The Golden Forest

Exploring a Coastal California Ecosystem

Written by
Carol Blanchette & Jenifer Dugan

Illustrations by Michael Rothman

muddy boots™

we jump in puddles

Lanham · New York · Boulder · Toronto · London

"Welcome to California!" Neko shouts. She throws her arms around her favorite cousin, who has traveled all the way from the Rocky Mountains of Colorado to see her.

"Thanks!" Owen says. "I can't wait to get to the ocean!"

2

3

At the beach, Owen is in awe of the big, blue ocean in front of him. Then suddenly, he hears a loud splash.

"What was that?" he shouts.

"Oh, that was just a pelican going fishing," says Neko. "Pelicans look for fish from the air. When they see one, they dive straight down underneath the water and scoop it up with their large bills."

"Cool!" Owen says, watching the big bird fly away with its prize.

4

5

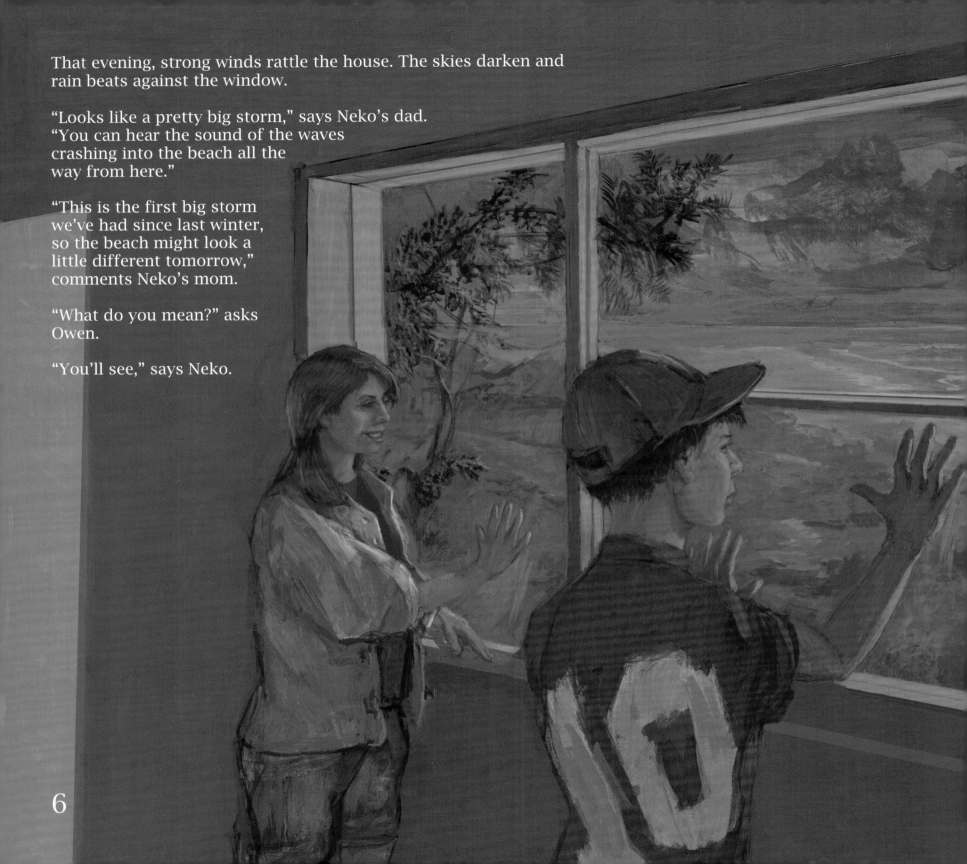

That evening, strong winds rattle the house. The skies darken and rain beats against the window.

"Looks like a pretty big storm," says Neko's dad. "You can hear the sound of the waves crashing into the beach all the way from here."

"This is the first big storm we've had since last winter, so the beach might look a little different tomorrow," comments Neko's mom.

"What do you mean?" asks Owen.

"You'll see," says Neko.

6

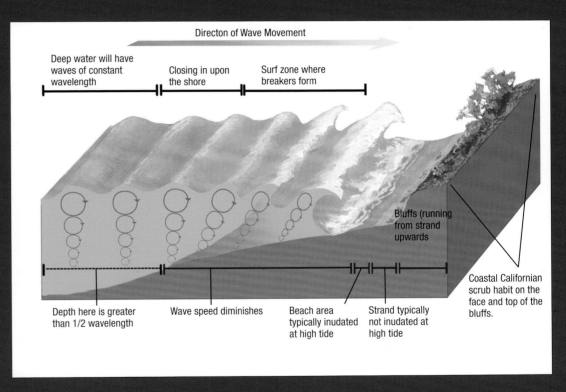

Directon of Wave Movement

Deep water will have waves of constant wavelength

Closing in upon the shore

Surf zone where breakers form

Bluffs (running from strand upwards

Depth here is greater than 1/2 wavelength

Wave speed diminishes

Beach area typically inudated at high tide

Strand typically not inudated at high tide

Coastal Californian scrub habit on the face and top of the bluffs.

Storms and Waves

As wind blows across the surface of the ocean, energy is transferred to the water. The friction between the air molecules and the water molecules causes energy to be transferred from the wind to the water. This causes waves to form. The water doesn't actually travel with the wave, but only moves up and down. It's the energy that travels with the wave. As the waves move closer to shore that energy can move sand, rocks, and organisms from the ocean onto the beach.

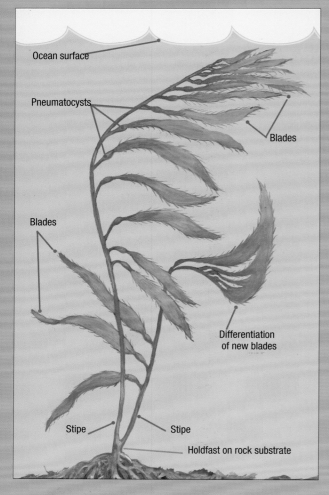

Ocean surface

Pneumatocysts

Blades

Blades

Differentiation
of new blades

Stipe   Stipe

Holdfast on rock substrate

Kelp

Although kelp looks like a plant, it belongs to a group of organisms called algae. Algae do not have true roots, stems, or leaves. Instead of roots, kelp has a branching structure called a holdfast that grows over rocks on the sea floor. Unlike roots, holdfasts do not take in nutrients. The main purpose of the holdfast is to keep the kelp from floating away. Rising up from a kelp's holdfast is a stem-like structure called a stipe. The stipe is strong and flexible. Flat, leaf-like blades grow out of the stipe. Blades use sunlight to make food for the kelp. They also absorb nutrients directly from the water. Kelp stipes and blades cannot stand up on their own. Gas-filled, ball-shaped "floats" called pneumatocysts pull the stipes and blades toward the sunlit surface.

8

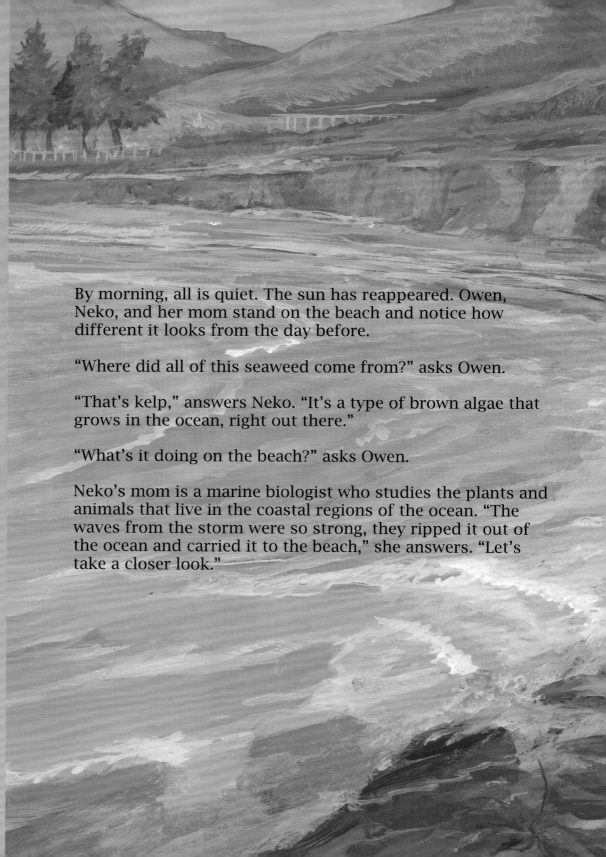

By morning, all is quiet. The sun has reappeared. Owen, Neko, and her mom stand on the beach and notice how different it looks from the day before.

"Where did all of this seaweed come from?" asks Owen.

"That's kelp," answers Neko. "It's a type of brown algae that grows in the ocean, right out there."

"What's it doing on the beach?" asks Owen.

Neko's mom is a marine biologist who studies the plants and animals that live in the coastal regions of the ocean. "The waves from the storm were so strong, they ripped it out of the ocean and carried it to the beach," she answers. "Let's take a closer look."

9

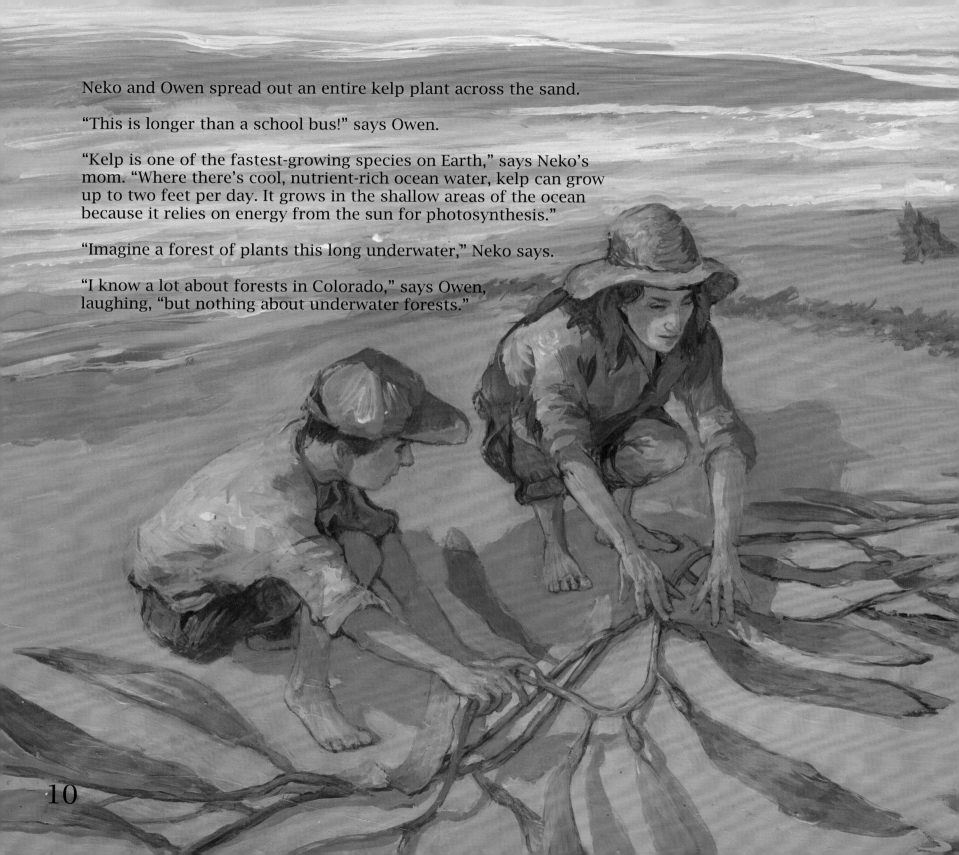

Neko and Owen spread out an entire kelp plant across the sand.

"This is longer than a school bus!" says Owen.

"Kelp is one of the fastest-growing species on Earth," says Neko's mom. "Where there's cool, nutrient-rich ocean water, kelp can grow up to two feet per day. It grows in the shallow areas of the ocean because it relies on energy from the sun for photosynthesis."

"Imagine a forest of plants this long underwater," Neko says.

"I know a lot about forests in Colorado," says Owen, laughing, "but nothing about underwater forests."

10

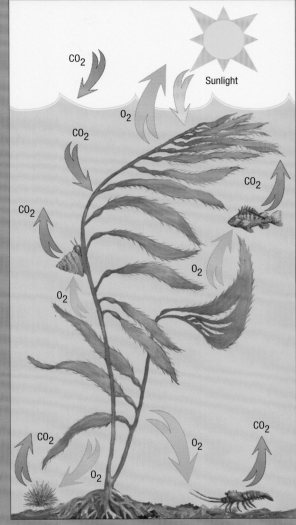

Photosynthesis

Although kelps resemble land plants, they are uniquely adapted to life in cool, clear, moving water. Kelp blades obtain energy from sunlight and take up carbon dioxide from water. Kelp blades use water and the energy from the sun to convert carbon dioxide to sugars and release oxygen into the water in a process called photosynthesis. The pneumatocysts of the kelp help to hold the blades close to the ocean surface, close to the sunlight.

11

"Let's see if you two are as strong as the waves that tore out these kelp plants," Neko's mom says.

"Sure! Let's try to pull them apart!" says Owen.

"Each kelp plant is made up of many separate strings, called stipes," says Neko's mom. "Neko, hold this end of the stipe, and Owen, you grab the other end."

"Now pull!" yells Neko. They pull on the kelp until the stipe breaks and they tumble onto the sand.

"Let's try three stipes!" says Neko.

This time, no matter how hard they pull, they can't break all three.

"That settles it," says Neko's mom, chuckling. "Ocean waves are stronger than you two!"

"What happens after a storm when the waves tear out the kelp?" asks Owen.

"Most storms only tear out some of the kelp, and that creates space for more light to reach the bottom, allowing algae and smaller kelp plants to grow. The kelp torn from the ocean after a storm is called wrack. It's an important source of food for all the animals that live in the sand on the beach."

"There are animals on the beach?" exclaims Owen.

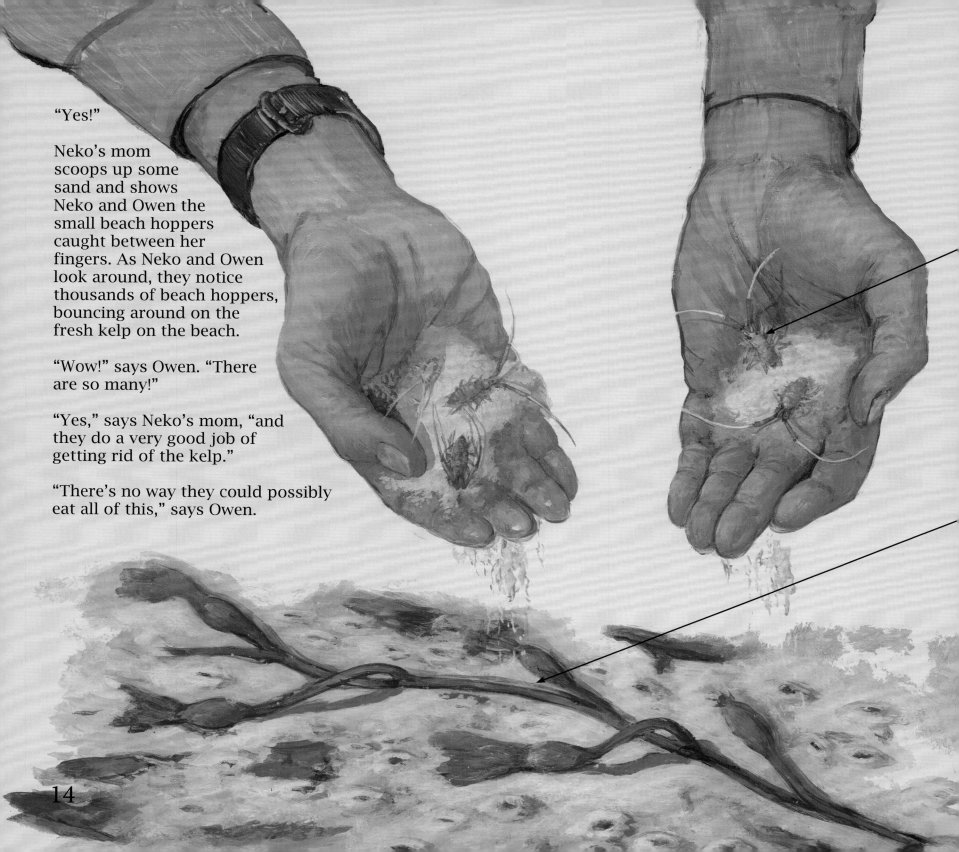

"Yes!"

Neko's mom scoops up some sand and shows Neko and Owen the small beach hoppers caught between her fingers. As Neko and Owen look around, they notice thousands of beach hoppers, bouncing around on the fresh kelp on the beach.

"Wow!" says Owen. "There are so many!"

"Yes," says Neko's mom, "and they do a very good job of getting rid of the kelp."

"There's no way they could possibly eat all of this," says Owen.

14

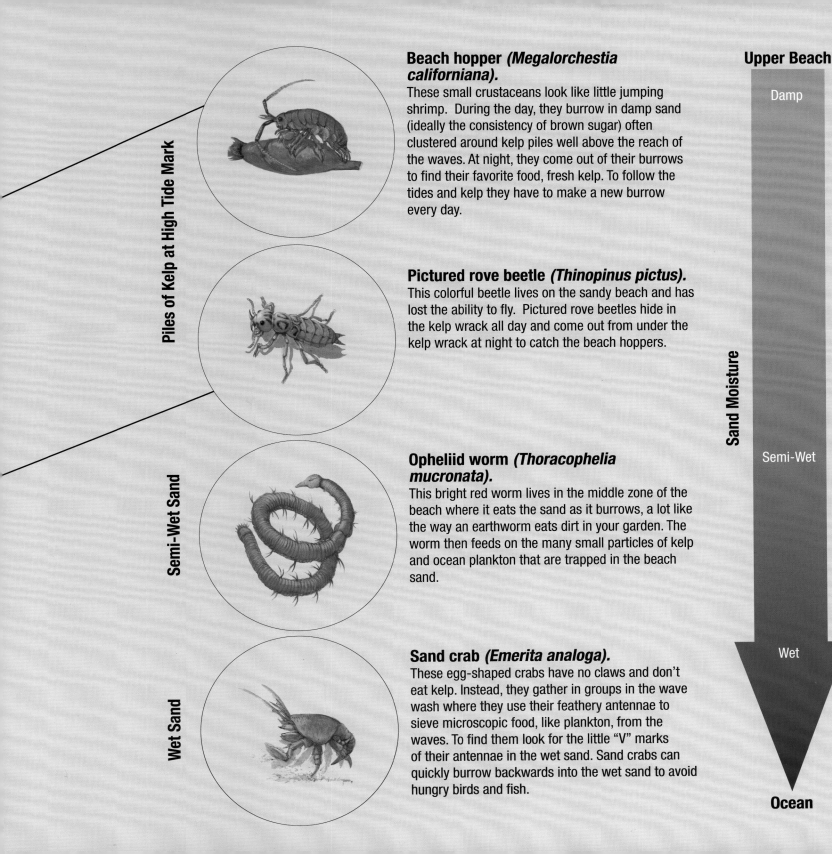

Piles of Kelp at High Tide Mark

Beach hopper *(Megalorchestia californiana).*

These small crustaceans look like little jumping shrimp. During the day, they burrow in damp sand (ideally the consistency of brown sugar) often clustered around kelp piles well above the reach of the waves. At night, they come out of their burrows to find their favorite food, fresh kelp. To follow the tides and kelp they have to make a new burrow every day.

Pictured rove beetle *(Thinopinus pictus).*

This colorful beetle lives on the sandy beach and has lost the ability to fly. Pictured rove beetles hide in the kelp wrack all day and come out from under the kelp wrack at night to catch the beach hoppers.

Semi-Wet Sand

Opheliid worm *(Thoracophelia mucronata).*

This bright red worm lives in the middle zone of the beach where it eats the sand as it burrows, a lot like the way an earthworm eats dirt in your garden. The worm then feeds on the many small particles of kelp and ocean plankton that are trapped in the beach sand.

Wet Sand

Sand crab *(Emerita analoga).*

These egg-shaped crabs have no claws and don't eat kelp. Instead, they gather in groups in the wave wash where they use their feathery antennae to sieve microscopic food, like plankton, from the waves. To find them look for the little "V" marks of their antennae in the wet sand. Sand crabs can quickly burrow backwards into the wet sand to avoid hungry birds and fish.

Upper Beach

Damp

Sand Moisture

Semi-Wet

Wet

Ocean

15

"I have an idea!" says Neko. "Let's do an experiment to find out how much wrack these little guys can actually eat."

She finds a stipe with several blades, and pulls it away from the pile.

"Let's lay out all the kelp blades flat on the sand; then we can come back later, find the same spot, and see how much wrack is left," she says.

Owen marks the location of their experiment with a shell and some driftwood, so they can be sure to find it the next day.

16

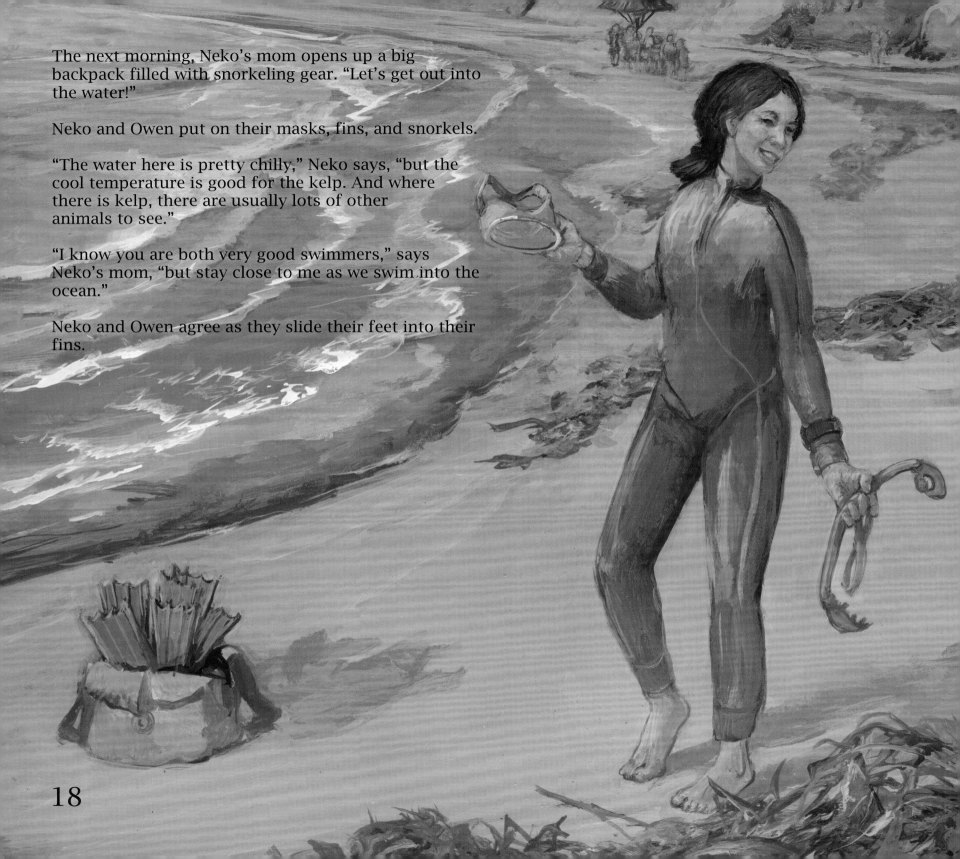

The next morning, Neko's mom opens up a big backpack filled with snorkeling gear. "Let's get out into the water!"

Neko and Owen put on their masks, fins, and snorkels.

"The water here is pretty chilly," Neko says, "but the cool temperature is good for the kelp. And where there is kelp, there are usually lots of other animals to see."

"I know you are both very good swimmers," says Neko's mom, "but stay close to me as we swim into the ocean."

Neko and Owen agree as they slide their feet into their fins.

18

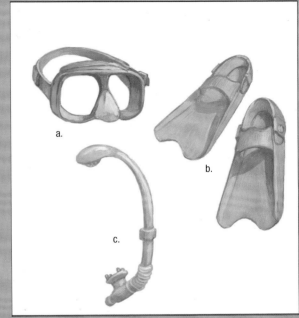

Snorkeling

Snorkeling is a way to observe organisms underwater, while breathing through a tube (the snorkel). Snorkeling in the cool waters off the coast of California typically requires a wetsuit, which is an outfit made out of neoprene that provides both thermal insulation and buoyancy. A diving mask is very important to provide visibility underwater. Fins, which are worn on the feet, provide more surface area for kicking and aid the movement through the water. The snorkel is the breathing tube, which provides a way to look underwater and breath air at the same time.

    a. Mask
    b. Fins
    c. Snorkel

The ocean bottom is full of life and color. A red spiny lobster pokes its antennae out from underneath a rock. Pink coralline algae, red algae, and green surfgrass cover much of the bottom surface. In between the algae the snorkelers see purple and red urchins and colorful sea stars, as well as crabs, sea cucumbers, and many more animals they have never seen before.

SPECIES KEY

1. Coralline algae *(Calliarthron cheilosporioides)*
2. Giant green anemone *(Anthopleura xanthanogrammica)*
3. Orange puff sponge *(Tethya californiana)*
4. Giant spined sea star *(Pisaster giganteus)*
5. Black surf perch *(Embiotica jacksoni)*
6. Surf grass *(Phyllospadix torreyi)*
7. Feather boa kelp *(Egregia menziesii)*
8. Green sea lettuce *(Ulva lactuca)*
9. Red algae *(Chrondracanthus corymbiferus)*
10. Purple sea urchin *(Stronglyocentrotus pupuratus)*
11. Red sea urchin *(Mesocentrotus franciscanus)*
12. California spiny lobster *(Panulirus interruptus)*
13. Garibaldi *(Hypsypops rubicundus)*
14. Crustose coralline algae (multiple species)
15. Colonial tunicates *(Botrylloides diegensis)*

21

Just beyond the surfgrass, a golden forest of kelp comes into view. The water near the kelp is deeper, so the swimmers kick with their fins to get closer to the bottom. They are surrounded by towers of golden kelp.

Sunlight streams between the stipes, and darting in and around the kelp are small golden fish called señoritas. Several rockfish stay close to the kelp, bobbing up and down with each passing wave. Below them a small leopard shark swims around, looking for crabs to eat. They catch glimpses of sea lions playing hide and seek in the golden forest.

When they return to the beach, Neko and Owen cannot stop talking about how many new and different creatures they saw.

"Do you think all of those creatures would be there without kelp?" asks Owen.

"Probably not as many," says Neko's mom.

"The kelp forest provides a protective habitat for animals that might be more easily found and eaten by predators without a good place to hide. The algae within the kelp forest also provide food for animals called grazers, such as urchins, snails, and abalone."

"Just like wrack provides food for the beach hoppers," adds Neko. "Hey, let's go check on our experiment!"

Neko and Owen race over to the shell and piece of driftwood marking the kelp they laid out on the beach the day before.

"Wow!" exclaims Owen. "It's almost gone. All that's left is part of the stipe! And look at all the beach hopper burrows where the blades of kelp used to be."

26

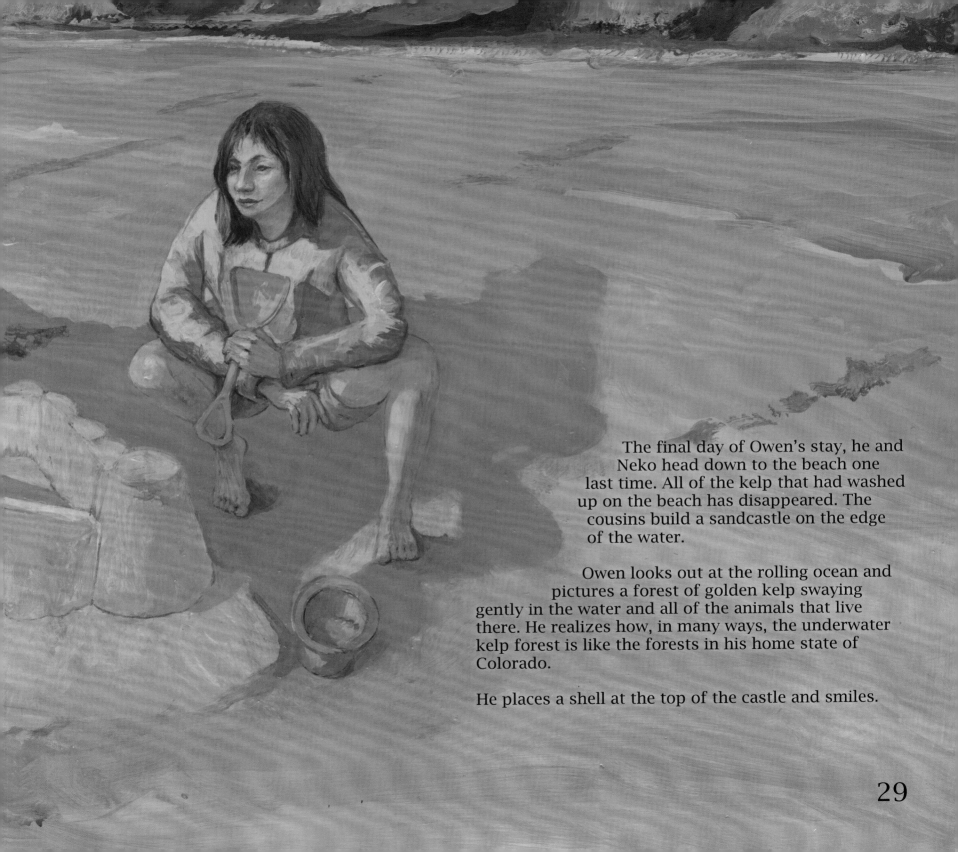

The final day of Owen's stay, he and
Neko head down to the beach one
last time. All of the kelp that had washed
up on the beach has disappeared. The
cousins build a sandcastle on the edge
of the water.

Owen looks out at the rolling ocean and
pictures a forest of golden kelp swaying
gently in the water and all of the animals that live
there. He realizes how, in many ways, the underwater
kelp forest is like the forests in his home state of
Colorado.

He places a shell at the top of the castle and smiles.

29

Glossary

Blades:
The flattened, leaf-like parts of kelp.

Driftwood:
Wood that has been washed onto the shore by the action of winds, tides, or waves.

Experiment:
A procedure carried out to verify, refute, or validate a hypothesis.

Grazers:
Animals that feed on plants or algae.

Habitat:
The place or environment where a plant or animal naturally or normally lives and grows.

Haptera:
The finger-like extensions of the holdfast that anchor kelp to the ocean floor.

Holdfast:
A specialized structure at the base of kelp that attaches it to the ocean floor.

Organisms:
Individual living things.

Pelican:
A type of seabird that has a long beak and a large throat pouch used for catching prey and draining water from the scooped up contents before swallowing.

Photosynthesis:
The process by which plants and algae, like kelp, use sunlight to produce energy.

Pneumatocysts:
The gas-filled floats on kelp that help to provide buoyancy.

Snorkeling:
The practice of swimming on or through a body of water while equipped with a diving mask, a shaped tube called a snorkel (used for breathing), and usually fins.

Stipes:
The stem-like parts of kelp.

Wetsuits:
Garments, usually made of foamed neoprene, worn by people engaged in water sports, such as snorkeling and diving, to provide thermal insulation in cold water.

Wrack:
Seaweeds and seagrasses that are found washed up onto the shore.

Things You Can Do to Keep the Ocean Healthy

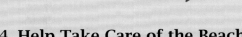

1. Reduce Energy Consumption

Reduce the effects of climate change on the ocean by choosing to walk when you can and being conscious of your energy use at home and school. For example, turn off lights when no one is using them and hang clothes outside to dry instead of using the clothes dryer.

2. Make Sustainable Seafood Choices

When shopping or dining out, help reduce the demand for overexploited species by choosing seafood that is both healthful and sustainable. You can learn more about which types of seafood are sustainable at www.seafoodwatch.org.

3. Use Fewer Plastic Products

To limit the amount of plastics that end up as ocean debris, carry a reusable water bottle, store food in non-disposable containers, bring your own cloth tote or other reusable bag when shopping, and recycle whenever possible.

4. Help Take Care of the Beach

Whether you enjoy diving, surfing, or relaxing on the beach, always clean up after yourself. Explore and appreciate the ocean without interfering with wildlife or removing rocks and organisms. Go even further by encouraging others to respect the marine environment or by participating in local beach cleanups.

5. Be an Ocean-Friendly Pet Owner

Never flush cat litter, which can contain pathogens harmful to marine life. Avoid stocking your aquarium with wild-caught saltwater fish, and never release any aquarium fish into the ocean or other bodies of water, which can introduce non-native species harmful to the existing ecosystem.

Published by Muddy Boots
An imprint of Globe Pequot
MuddyBootsBooks.com

Distributed by NATIONAL BOOK NETWORK

Copyright © 2017 Carol Blanchette
& Jenifer Dugan

Illustrations © 2017 Michael Rothman

British Library Cataloguing-in-Publication
Information available

Library of Congress Cataloguing-in-
Publication Information available

ISBN 978-1-63076-180-6 (hardback)
ISBN 978-1-63076-181-3 (e-book)

Printed in China

This material is based upon work
supported by the National Science
Foundation under grant no. DEB 1624129.
Any opinions, findings, and conclusions
or recommendations expressed in this
material are those of the author and do not
necessarily reflect the view of the National
Science Foundation.

About the Long Term Ecological Research (LTER) Network

The LTER Network is a large-scale program supported by the National Science Foundation. It consists of 25 ecological research projects, each of which is focused on a different ecosystem. The goals of the LTER Network are:

Understanding: To understand a diverse array of ecosystems at multiple spatial and temporal scales.

Synthesis: To create general knowledge through long-term, interdisciplinary research, synthesis of information, and development of theory.

Information: To inform the LTER and broader scientific community by creating well-designed and well-documented databases.

Legacies: To create a legacy of well designed and documented long-term observations, experiments, and archives of samples and specimens for future generations.

Education: To promote training, teaching, and learning about long-term ecological research and the Earth's ecosystems, and to educate a new generation of scientists.

Outreach: To reach out to the broader scientific community, natural resource managers, policymakers, and the general public by providing decision support, information, recommendations, and the knowledge and capability to address complex environmental challenges.

About the Santa Barbara Coastal LTER

The Santa Barbara Coastal Long Term Ecological Research Project (SBC) is housed at the University of California, Santa Barbara (UCSB) and is part of the National Science Foundation's (NSF) Long Term Ecological Research (LTER) Network. Giant kelp (Macrocystis pyrifera) forests are located at the land-ocean margin in temperate regions of both the northern and southern hemispheres, and represent one of the most productive ecosystems in the world. The primary research objective of the SBC LTER is to investigate the relative importance of land and ocean processes in structuring giant kelp forest ecosystems.

Acknowledgements

Funding for *The Golden Forest* was provided by the US National Science Foundation under grants OCE 9982105, 0620276 and 1232779 to the Santa Barbara Coastal LTER. We would also like to acknowledge the UCSB Marine Science Institute, the Partnership for Interdisciplinary Studies of Coastal Oceans and the Math Science Partnership. We would like to acknowledge the following individuals; Dan Reed, Sally Holbrook, David Hubbard, Scott Simon, Andrew Brooks, Katherine Emery, Shannon Harrer and Clint Nelson.

Dedications

To my family, particularly my grandparents Tony and Agnes, for inspiring my love of the ocean, and my daughter Neko who leads me in a new adventure in nature everyday.
~CB

To my salty, sandy family, especially my husband, Dave.
~JD

To my daughter Nyanza and my wife Dorothy.
~MR